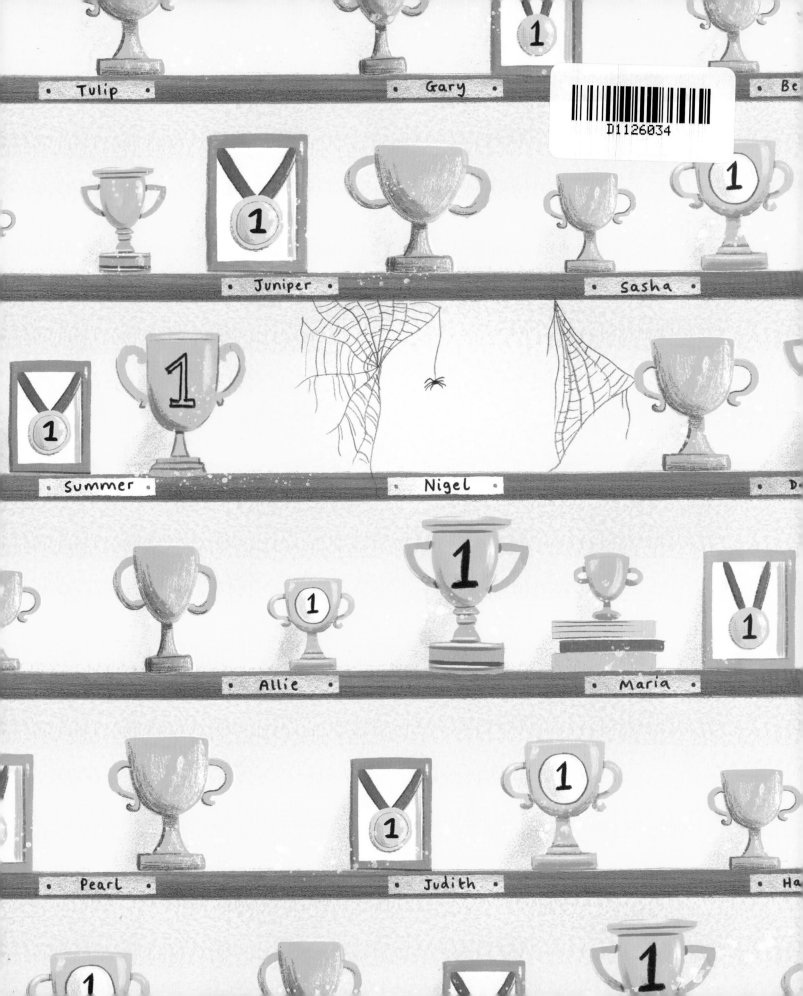

For Scarlett and Tabitha

First US edition 2022
First published by Templar Books, an imprint of Bonnier Books UK, 2020

Library of Congress Catalog Card Number 2021947417
ISBN 978-1-5362-2386-6

22 23 24 25 26 27 TLF 10 9 8 7 6 5 4 3 2 1

Printed in Dongguan, Guangdong, China

This book was typeset in Trocchi.
The illustrations were done in gouache and
colored pencil and with digital painting.

TEMPLAR BOOKS
an imprint of
Candlewick Press
99 Dover Street
Somerville, Massachusetts 02144

www.candlewick.com

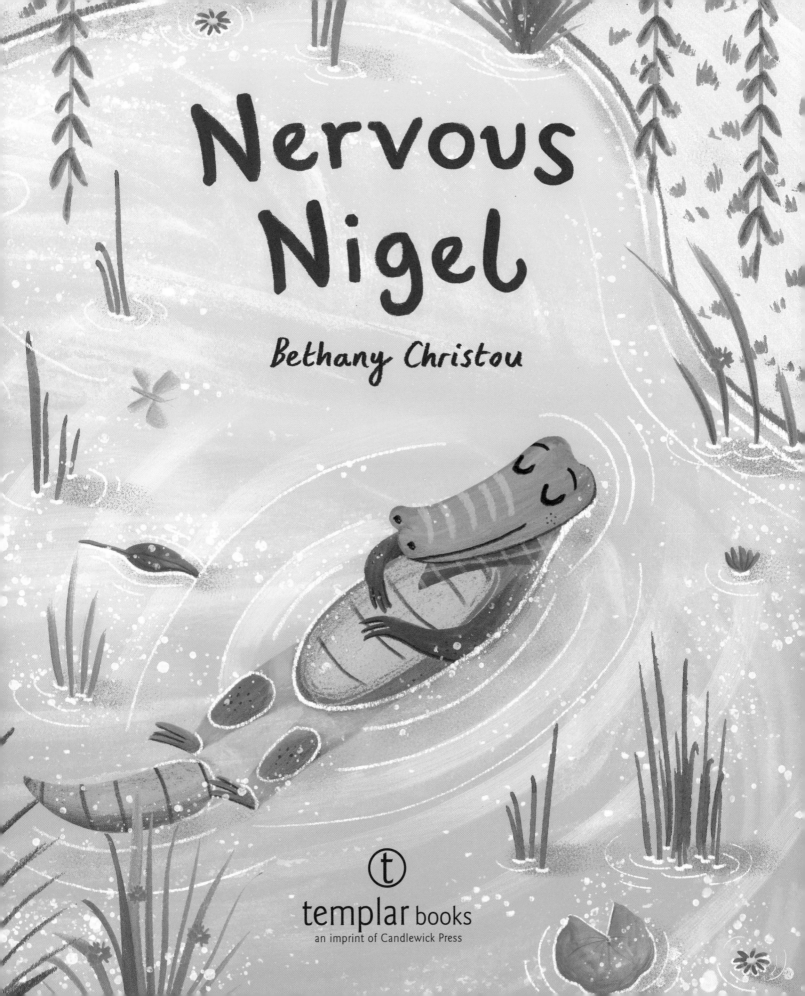

Nervous
Nigel

Bethany Christou

templar books
an imprint of Candlewick Press

Nigel came from
a long line of greats.

Every crocodile in his family was a champion.

Nigel's mom was the fastest swimmer in crocodile history.

JUNIPER
RECORD BREAKER, REPTILE WORLD CHAMPIONSHIP

GRANNY LOU
GOLD MEDAL, BACKSTROKE, CROC GAMES

His sister Summer could win marathons with her eyes shut.

SUMMER
FIRST PLACE, RIVER NILE HALF MARATHON

Nigel's other sister, Bonnie, was the first crocodile to get a perfect diving score . . .

BONNIE
Gold, diving, Junior Croc Games

and his brother, Ralf, was captain of the water polo team.

RALF
Snap School Water Polo Team

Nigel's family wanted him to be a champion swimmer.
And Nigel *did* love swimming.

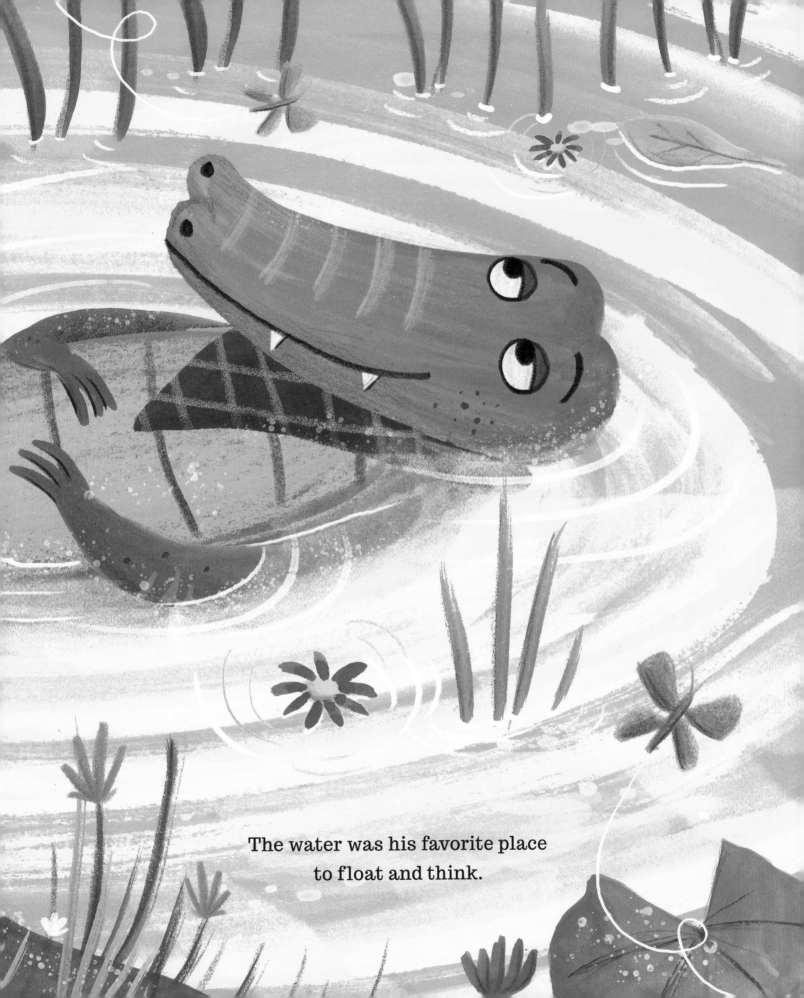

The water was his favorite place
to float and think.

But as soon as Nigel started training,
being in the water didn't seem fun anymore.

Once the whistle blew,
his heart started **thumping.**

GO! GO! GO!

When the shouting got louder,
his teeth started **chattering.**

FASTER!

As his mom shouted,
his tail started *trembling*.

But he couldn't tell
his mom how he felt,
so he always said . . .

That was a
lovely swim!

Then, one day, his family told him
they'd entered him in his first competition.

Nigel began to **panic**.

I... But... It's just...

His heart started **thumping**.
His tail started *trembling*.
His teeth started **chattering**.

But he couldn't let his family know,
so all he said was . . .

That night, Nigel couldn't sleep. His head was full of all the **terrible things** that could happen.

Nigel decided that he had to get out of the competition.

But no matter what he tried—

and he tried a LOT of things—

nothing seemed to work.

There was only one thing left to do,
and that was tell the truth.

Nigel had to let his family know how he felt.

Heart **thumping**, tail *trembling*,
teeth **chattering**, Nigel approached
the kitchen door.

He asked, "What would you think if a crocodile *didn't* want to be a champion?"

His family was bewildered.

Nigel's mom and brother and sisters did
their best to reassure him.

But nothing made him feel better,
and soon Nigel wished he hadn't said anything at all.

The day of the competition arrived.

And even though he tried to hide it,

Nigel was **shaking** with nervousness.

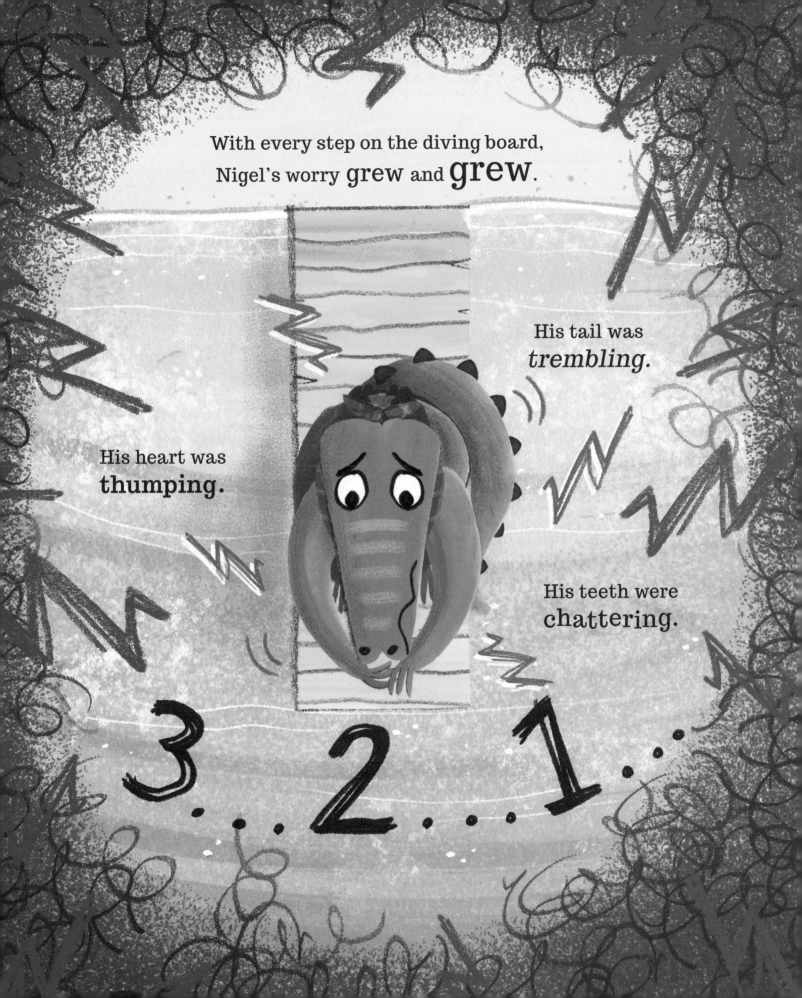

With every step on the diving board,
Nigel's worry grew and **grew**.

His tail was
trembling.

His heart was
thumping.

His teeth were
chattering.

3... 2... 1...

Finally, Nigel couldn't hide it any longer.
He was too nervous to race.

Nigel's family rushed over to him.
Nigel was certain that he'd disappointed them.

Nigel...

He ran off before they
could say anything else.

Farther down the river, Nigel did
his best to forget what had happened.
Floating usually helped him feel calm,
but today he just felt lost.

Then, he heard
a little voice . . .

Excuse me?

It was a frog. She asked Nigel to give her a ride across the water.

Nigel was only too pleased to help.

The frog thought Nigel looked sad, so she
asked him what the problem was. Nigel told her.

But the frog didn't agree.

And that gave Nigel a brilliant idea . . .

Nigel's Floating Ferry and Scenic Tours was a **great** success.

Nigel didn't need to rush
or race, and he didn't have to
worry or lose sleep.

Now he could float
and think all he liked.

BOOK
HERE
←

And it seemed that lots
of other animals liked
to do the same.

Nigel wasn't winning any medals,
but he was doing something he loved.